BY
CHRISSIE PERRY

ILLUSTRATIONS BY
DANIELLE McDONALD

BASED ON ORIGINAL ILLUSTRATIONS
BY ASH OSWALD

Lucky Stars
published in 2007 by
Hardie Grant Egmont
85 High Street
Prahran, Victoria 3181, Australia

A CiP record for this title is available from the National Library of Australia

Text copyright © 2007 Chrissie Perry
Illustration and design copyright © 2007 Hardie Grant Egmont
The moral rights of the author have been asserted

Design and cover by Ash Oswald
Internal illustrations by Danielle McDonald
Based on original illustrations by Ash Oswald
Typesetting by Pauline Haas

Printed in Australia by McPherson's Printing Group

3 5 7 9 10 8 6 4 2

PREVIOUSLY ON...

Go Girl! Angels

The Angels' dog wash was a big success.
But there's still one more challenge to go.
There have been highs and lows,
but the Angels are really working
together like a team now.

Will Lucy remember there's no 'I' in 'team'
and help the Angels take centre stage?

CHAPTER One

Lucy stacked all the beanbags in the corner. She packed up her magazines, and put them away on the shelves. Then she took all the glasses and plates back to the kitchen.

I don't think the playroom has ever looked this tidy! Lucy thought.

It was Saturday afternoon, and the Angels were coming over to Lucy's house. They were going to need lots of space.

Finally, *finally*, they were up to the performance challenge, and Lucy was ready to be the perfect leader.

The other challenges have been great!

Lucy thought back over the other Team Terrific challenges they'd done. The soccer game had been awesome. She couldn't help giggling when she remembered the Angels falling into the pool during the raft race.

And even though Mrs Clarke said that the Help Others challenge was a draw, Lucy still thought the Angels' dog wash had been the winner!

The last challenge had been hard, though. Lucy had half-expected Chloe to ruin it with her short temper, but the Angels had come through it fine.

Actually, Lucy thought, *the Angels keep getting better at working together!* Everyone was getting on really well, and Chloe seemed fine now that Bonnie had chosen Lucy as the leader of the final challenge. That was definitely a relief!

Lucy felt as though she knew all the Angels really well now. The performance was going to be the best challenge yet. Lucy could feel it in her bones.

When the doorbell rang, Lucy charged madly up the stairs and down the corridor to the front door.

This is going to be a GREAT practice!

'Hi, Angels!' she yelled. It was great that they'd all got a lift from Sophie's dad. It meant that they would be starting practice right on time.

'Hi, Luce,' the other Angels yelled back.

'Hey, cool house,' Sophie added.

'Thanks, Soph,' she replied. 'Now, Angels, follow me.'

Lucy couldn't help skipping as she headed back down the corridor with the Angels behind her. As she turned around, she noticed everyone else was skipping too! Well, everyone except for Chloe. But that was understandable – her arm was in a sling. Sometimes Chloe lost her balance. Lucy had already planned out the routine so that Chloe had some easy dance moves.

'Hey, whose room is this?' Annabelle asked.

Lucy looked over her shoulder. All the other Angels had stopped outside Frankie's closed door. Loud music thumped through the gaps.

'Oh, that's just Frankie's room,' Bonnie said, making her voice loud enough to be heard over the music.

'She's my big sister,' Lucy explained.

'Wow, where did she get those cool stickers?' Lola asked, pointing to Frankie's decorated door.

Lucy shrugged. She actually didn't like the stickers on Frankie's door very much. All of them seemed to be directed at her!

Chloe came up behind Lucy, bumping her on the arm with her cast as she stopped walking. 'My big sister Ashley is a total meanie,' she said. 'Is yours?'

Lucy crinkled up her nose. That was a hard question to answer. Sometimes Frankie was a meanie. But other times she was actually pretty nice.

'Frankie's OK, I guess,' Lucy said. 'Most of the time.'

Lucy's thoughts drifted away from the Angels and onto Frankie. She'd been so busy with school work and the Team Terrific challenges that she'd barely thought about what was happening with Frankie. Or maybe she'd been trying *not* to think about it.

Frankie was going to Spain in just one week. She was actually leaving straight after the Angels did their performance. She was going on a student exchange, and she was going to be away for a whole year!

'Come on,' Lucy urged, heading down the hallway and sliding down the banister.

Now was definitely not the time to start thinking about Frankie leaving. 'Let's practise.'

CHAPTER Two

'I found the *best* song in mum's old CD collection,' Lucy said excitedly. 'I really think it will be perfect to dance to.'

'Put it on,' Bonnie urged.

'It's called *Girls Just Wanna Have Fun*,' said Lucy, as she put the disc in the CD player and pressed play. She watched the Angels' faces as they listened.

'This song rocks!' Chloe said, tapping her foot to the beat.

'Yeah, it's like it was made just for the Angels,' Lola giggled.

'*Angels, they want, wanna have fun,*' Annabelle sang loudly, making up her own lyrics to the song.

Lucy grinned. 'So, who wants to use it for our performance?' she asked, laughing as *everyone* put up their hands. She was totally rapt that all the Angels liked the song as much as she did. Even if it was an old song, Girls Just Wanna Have Fun was still really cool and dancy. There were plenty of great moves Lucy had learnt in dance class that would work with the beat.

'OK, I'll play it again,' she said, feeling confident. It was funny how dancing always made her feel so great.

'This time, we should stand in three rows of two. I'll stand up the front with Lola.' Lucy pointed to a place on the floor where she and Lola could dance. 'Next row, Annabelle and Sophie,' she directed. 'And then Chloe and Bonnie at the back.'

'Hey, why do we have to go up the back?' Chloe asked.

Lucy bit her lip. 'Well,' she said slowly, 'I'm going to give you guys some easy moves to do at the back. I thought that would be easier for you with your arm in a sling. And Bonnie ... well, Bonnie's not really that . . .' Suddenly, Lucy found herself searching for the right words.

Bonnie found some before she did. 'I'm not a good dancer,' she said.

Lucy didn't like the way Bonnie's voice was kind of small as she said it. It made her feel a bit bad. But the performance was really important. Bonnie would understand.

'OK, we'll do the easy steps first. Follow me,' Lucy instructed. She started the music from the beginning.

'Step behind, step kick,' she called out as she did the actions. 'Step behind, step clap.'

Lucy turned around as she called and danced. Sophie and Annabelle were doing well. Chloe was really good, too . . . well,

except for the clap. Maybe Lucy would have to think of something else to go there. But Bonnie ... Lucy sighed as Bonnie tripped over her own feet. She was really glad she'd cleaned up the playroom!

'OK, let's try again,' Lucy said. She made sure all the Angels were in their

proper places, and restarted the music.
Then she heard a creak as the playroom
door opened.

'How's it going, Angels?' Lucy's mum
asked. She was carrying a tray of hot
chicken wings.

'Yum, Mrs B,' Bonnie said. 'Are these
with barbeque sauce?'

'Yep,' Lucy's mum said with a smile.
'Enjoy, Angels!'

Lucy's mum was always making Lucy
and Bonnie yummy after-school snacks.
Usually Lucy loved it. But right now, she
kind of wished her mum hadn't brought
snacks down to the playroom. The Angels
had a lot of work to do.

As Lucy's mum left the room, the Angels hovered around the tray. Lucy waited impatiently as the others devoured the food.

At least they're fast eaters, she thought. It wasn't long before the tray was empty.

Lucy put on the music again. 'OK, step behind, step ...' But then the playroom door creaked again!

'Keep going, Angels. Watch your feet,' she said. Lucy kept her eyes at floor level, checking out everyone's footwork. But someone else's feet were in there too. Frankie's strappy high heels! Purple toe-nails that exactly matched her fingernails peeped through the gaps of the shoes.

All the Angels stopped dancing.

'I've got a move you could do to this song,' Frankie said. She pulled out the elastic band from her hair and shook her hair over her shoulders. Lucy could see Frankie had been at the hair dye again. Frankie's hair was a different colour just about every time Lucy saw her! Right now, it was brown with big golden streaks through it.

Lucy sighed as the Angels watched her big sister. Frankie clicked her fingers. She did a grapevine, and swung her hair back at the end of the step. She was wearing a strapless top with a drifty skirt that flared up as she moved.

It was exactly the same step Lucy had shown them. Except for the hair flick.

'Wow,' Lola said softly. 'That was really good.'

'Can we try it?' Sophie asked, already pulling the elastic out of her hair. Annabelle swung her bob around.

'Of course you can,' Frankie said. 'OK, everyone, you do it like this . . .'

Lucy bit her lip as she watched the

Angels try to copy Frankie's move. The music rang out through the playroom.

None of the Angels had even noticed that Lucy wasn't joining in.

CHAPTER Three

'Watch out, Belle! Mrs Clarke is on the prowl,' Sophie said with a giggle. Annabelle put her sandwich back in her lunchbox and sat on her hands as Mrs Clarke walked by.

'That was close,' Annabelle laughed, stretching her polished fingernails out in front of her. Lucy rolled her eyes. The purple polish didn't even look that good. Annabelle had managed to paint the skin around her fingernails, too!

Lucy knew that Annabelle was trying to look like Frankie, but she didn't want to say anything about it. She definitely didn't want to start *another* conversation about how cool her big sister was!

Lucy tapped the pocket of her school skirt, where the CD was. She was glad she'd booked the multi-purpose room for practice today. At least this time there wouldn't be any interruptions from her mum or Frankie.

'How about we do a spin right here?' Chloe suggested. 'You know, when the music gets to . . .'

'Nah, let's just do it the way that Lucy said,' Bonnie interrupted.

Lucy saw Chloe breathe deeply, like she was trying not to get angry.

'That's a good suggestion, actually Chloe,' Lucy jumped in quickly. 'I think it might work, if you guys want to try it?' Lucy felt good as she saw Chloe's scowl turn into a grin.

This practice was going much, much better than the first one. So far, the Angels had figured out half the dance. And it really looked amazing.

Chloe and Bonnie were in the back row doing simple moves. Then Annabelle and Sophie in the next row were doing slightly more complicated moves. Lucy and Lola were in front, doing some great spins and jumps that Lucy had learnt in dance class.

'OK, one more time, Angels,' Lucy said.

The girls stepped and clapped. They whirled and jumped as the beat rocked the room. They swirled and swivelled ...

Bang! A stack of plastic chairs fell to the ground, clattering loudly.

'Are you OK, Bonnie?' Lucy asked, rushing over to her friend. Bonnie sat on the floor, rubbing her leg where she'd bumped into the stack.

'Yeah, I'm fine,' she said, smiling. 'It's just lucky you can hide me up the back. Otherwise, I'd ruin the whole dance!'

Lucy tilted her head to the side. Bonnie seemed to be smiling with her mouth. But her eyes looked ... well, they looked a little bit sad.

There must be a better way to do this!

Suddenly, Lucy found herself thinking about Bonnie and Chloe being stuck in the back row. Maybe there was another way to do the performance? *Maybe there's a way to camouflage Chloe's cast, and to help Bonnie's dancing?* Lucy wondered. She just had to figure out how to do it.

Lucy grabbed Bonnie's arm and helped her up as the bell rang.

'Excellent practice, Luce!' Sophie said.

'Yeah, we're great!' laughed Annabelle.

Lucy felt a smile creeping over her face. Even if there was still a bit to work out, things were going really well with the Angels' dance routine. And things were going well with the Angels generally, too!

Until Lola spoke.

'Hey, let's all go to Lucy's house tonight and see what Frankie thinks,' she said. 'We could show her our dance outfits, too!'

'Yeah, that'd be cool!' said Chloe.

All the Angels agreed.

All except for one – Lucy stayed silent.

CHAPTER Four

Lucy had thought a bit about what the Angels should wear for the performance. It was probably best that they all chose the coolest outfit they owned. It was the sort of song that needed everybody to dress individually. Lucy had asked the Angels to wear their favourite outfits.

Lucy had chosen her favourite pink shoes, which matched her favourite pink

T-shirt, and teamed them with a dark denim skirt. It hadn't been that hard to choose. Since her mum had bought her the clothes, it seemed like she never wanted to wear anything else!

Most of the Angels turned up in *really* groovy clothes. Lola looked cool in a black singlet with a silver star on it, and a matching black skirt. Bonnie looked awesome in flared jeans and a purple singlet. Annabelle looked cute in a blue halter-neck dress. Sophie rocked in green cargo pants and a white T-shirt.

But Lucy was a bit surprised when she saw Chloe. She wasn't going to be able to dance in those high heels! And she was wearing a strapless dress that looked like it might fall down.

Lucy bit her lip. Telling Chloe that her clothes and shoes weren't right would be really, really hard. In fact, Lucy didn't think she could do it without badly upsetting Chloe!

Lucy scratched her nose. Yep, it was better not to mention the clothes and shoes at all. It was better just to get on with practising.

Lucy started the music as everyone got into their places. Everything was going well. Bonnie wasn't quite in time, but at least she wasn't having any accidents. Chloe's high heels made her look a bit more wobbly than usual, but that didn't matter. Just as long as she didn't fall over!

Lucy felt out of breath when the song finished. That was their first full run-through. She imagined the audience clapping loudly. The Angels were *so* going to win the performance challenge!

'That was cool,' Sophie said, as though she was reading Lucy's mind.

'*Way* cool,' Lola added. 'We're going to be much better than the Devils. Did you hear they're doing a rap song that they made up themselves? They reckon they're *so* funny.'

'Like, duh,' Bonnie said. 'I mean, the Devils *are* funny. But they're *weird* funny, not *ha ha* funny!'

Everyone laughed. Only Annabelle was quiet. 'You know the Thunderbolts have formed their own band?' she said. 'I reckon they'll be pretty good. Maddy is awesome on guitar. Remember that time she played at assembly?'

'Hmm,' Lucy said. 'Well, we'll just have to be better.'

Suddenly, all the Angels went quiet.

'Let's get Frankie now, and show her the whole dance,' Annabelle suggested.

'Yeah, Frankie will tell us where we could improve,' Sophie said. 'If we're going to beat the Thunderbolts, we need to –'

'Frankie's not home,' Lucy said quickly. It was only a *little* fib.

'I'll just run up and check,' Bonnie replied. 'I think I heard someone moving about in her room.'

Lucy flopped onto a beanbag as the

other Angels trooped up to Frankie's room. It was really annoying how the Angels kept on wanting Frankie's opinion on everything. *I'm just as good at dancing,* Lucy thought irritably. *Aren't I?*

Lucy crossed her arms tightly as Frankie came into the playroom, surrounded by chattering Angels.

'Hey, Lou,' she said. 'How's the dance coming along?'

Lucy rolled her eyes. 'It's OK,' she mumbled back.

'What do you think of our clothes?' Annabelle asked excitedly.

Frankie smiled. 'All right, stand back,' she said, and then scratched her chin while she thought.

'Annabelle, that looks cool. Sophie, that's a good outfit for the song. Lou, Lola, Bon, you all look awesome . . .'

Then Frankie turned to look at Chloe,

her eyebrows raised in surprise. *Uh-oh,* Lucy thought.

'Um, Chloe, is that a dress or a skirt?' Frankie asked.

Lucy watched as Chloe's face turned bright red. The Angels all froze.

'Ah, I guess it's . . . it's really a skirt,' Chloe said softly, adjusting the elastic that stopped just under her arms. 'But I thought if I pulled it up high . . . I thought it looked a bit like your blue dress.' Chloe's voice had gone a bit wobbly.

Lucy held her breath. Part of her actually wanted Chloe to lose her temper. At least that might turn Frankie off interfering with the Angels all the time.

'You know what?' Frankie said brightly. 'It's great as a skirt, but you should *wear* it as a skirt. And I've got the perfect top you could match with it!'

Chloe's face lit up as Frankie ran off to get the top. Lucy stared at the carpet as Frankie came back with a bright blue ribbed singlet with a bird on the front in little diamond sequins.

'It's too small for me anyway, so you can have it,' Frankie said, handing the top to Chloe.

It was weird. Lucy had never really liked that top. But still, Frankie shouldn't be giving it to Chloe. She should be handing it down to her little sister!

Lucy's temper simmered as the Angels all admired the singlet. And it boiled as Chloe put the top on.

'OK, do you guys want me to watch your performance now?' Frankie asked, looking directly at Lucy.

Lucy was so angry, she felt like she was about to explode!

CHAPTER Five

'Frankie, don't you have something else you have to do?' Lucy asked.

'No . . .' Frankie replied slowly, shaking her head.

Lucy flicked her lip with her finger. 'Then don't you want to catch up with some of your *own* friends, since you're going away soon?'

Lucy glanced around the playroom. She could tell that the others thought she was being nasty. She breathed deeply and told herself she was doing the right thing. Frankie shouldn't be taking over like this. After all, Lucy was supposed to be organising the performance.

But as Frankie left, closing the playroom door softly behind her, Lucy felt a lump in her throat. Her head started to hurt. She pulled a beanbag out from the wall, and sat down.

'That was a bit mean,' Annabelle said. 'I think you hurt Frankie's feelings.'

Lucy rubbed her temples. Her headache was getting worse. Especially when she saw that Lola was crossing her arms and staring down at her. 'You'll miss Frankie when she goes away,' Lola said.

All the other Angels nodded firmly in agreement.

'How would you know?' Lucy blurted out. 'None of you even have sisters!'

No-one gets it!

'Well, I do,' Chloe said loudly. 'But she's not nice like —'

Suddenly, Lucy got up. It was none of their business what she said to Frankie! 'Anyway, let's just think about the performance,' Lucy said, trying to take the wobble out of her voice. 'Let's go from the first chorus again . . .'

'Actually,' Chloe began, 'my arm's hurting. I think I'd better give my dad a call to pick me up.'

'Yeah, I'm pretty tired,' Lola added.

Before she knew it, everyone except for Bonnie had left. The two of them slumped into matching beanbags.

'Don't worry about it, Lou,' Bonnie

said kindly. 'I'm much meaner to Boofhead and Pinhead sometimes.'

Lucy put her head into her hands. 'I *am* going to miss her,' she said softly. 'I still can't believe she's actually going. It's just ...'

It's true – I will miss Frankie

'I know,' Bonnie sighed. She grabbed one of Lucy's hands, and held it tight.

All of the things Lucy had tried not to think about danced around in her head. Frankie was going away for a whole year! That meant a whole year of being alone. A whole year of Frankie's room being empty. A whole year of not having to share their bathroom, of not arguing about who got the token out of the breakfast cereal packets. A whole year of –

Suddenly, the pause button clicked off on the CD player, and music filled up the room.

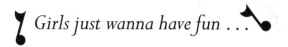 *Girls just wanna have fun . . .*

Lucy bit her lip. A tear trickled down her cheek. She *did* want to have fun.

But it wasn't turning out that way.

Not at all.

CHAPTER Six

Lucy looked around the corridor outside her classroom. Ms Diamond had just finished putting up some amazing photos of the Use Your Brain challenge. The photos of the Angels team were very funny. They told the whole story of the raft race in pictures!

In the first photo, the Angels were winning the race and Bonnie was standing

Hey, funny photos!

up on the raft, grinning and waving her arms around. In the second, the Angels' raft was upside down, and the Angels were bobbing around in the pool!

Everyone walked around from photo to photo, laughing and talking. Lucy giggled as she looked at a photo of the Devils splashing into the swimming pool. Bits of their raft were flung around them in the water!

'OK, back inside the classroom, please,' Ms Diamond called out.

Lucy went inside and returned to her seat.

'I'd like to say that I'm proud of all of you,' Ms Diamond said. 'You all seem to be working very well on Team Terrific. I just wondered whether you would like to share some ideas about what you've learnt so far.'

Lucy saw Bonnie shoot up her hand. It had taken a while, but Bonnie had *finally* learnt not to call out in Ms Diamond's class.

Ms Diamond nodded at her. 'I learnt that you shouldn't stand up and dance when you're on a raft!' Bonnie said, *giggling*.

Everyone laughed. Lucy grinned at her friend.

'True,' said Ms Diamond, with a smile. 'Is there anything else you've learnt? Maybe something about teamwork?'

Lucy watched Maddy as she arched her back to reach her hand up high into the air.

'Maddy?' Ms Diamond said.

'It's not easy to work as a team,' Maddy said thoughtfully. 'But the most important thing about being part of a team is trying to be fair to everyone.'

'Very good,' Ms Diamond said, nodding. 'Does anyone have anything else to add?'

Lucy scratched her neck. She saw

other hands shoot up. It was good how Ms Diamond let the class have these discussions. This time, she picked Joey.

'Everyone should get an equal turn at things,' Joey said. 'Like, it's not fair if some people get all the turns.'

Lucy turned to look out the window. What Maddy and Joey had said was true.

Lucy felt herself thinking about the Angels' dance routine again. Maybe it wasn't fair that Bonnie and Chloe were shoved up the back? Maybe giving everyone different dance moves wasn't actually giving everyone an equal turn?

Lucy closed her eyes for a second. She had a great idea! She could see it all in her mind – all of the Angels should be doing exactly the same moves, and Chloe and Bonnie should go in the middle!

That way, Bonnie could copy everyone's steps and Chloe could camouflage her cast *without* feeling left out. Sophie and Annabelle could have a turn at the front, too. And it didn't matter if Lucy wasn't doing the cool moves that she'd learnt in dance class – it would look even cooler if they were all dancing in unison. They would *really* look like a team!

The more she thought about it, the more Lucy knew it would work. In fact, it would look even better than it did before! Lucy grinned happily.

But Lucy still felt bad about what she'd said to Frankie. There had been no time to talk to her about what had happened in the playroom – Frankie had gone out with her friends all evening.

But at least she had an idea that might make two people a bit happier. She couldn't wait to tell Bonnie and Chloe!

'Are you sure?' Bonnie asked doubtfully, as the Angels gathered together.

'Of course she's sure!' Chloe replied. 'It's a great idea. We can try it out right now.'

Lucy smiled as the Angels stood in their new dance formation. They were right at the back of the oval where no-one could see them. They didn't have a CD player on the oval, but by now the Angels knew the song they were dancing to so well they could sing it in their sleep.

Lucy smiled as they all sung and danced. Turning to look behind her, Lucy could see that Bonnie was keeping up. In fact, she was

dancing much better than she had before, because now she could just follow everyone else's moves. Lucy loved seeing the grin on Bonnie's face as she yelled out the lyrics. She loved it even more when both Chloe and Bonnie gave her the thumbs-up sign!

When they'd finished, all the Angels collapsed on the ground, laughing and catching their breath.

'The Angels are awesome!' Sophie giggled, trying to tickle Annabelle.

'Yep. We totally rock!' Lola added. 'We're going to blow everyone away tomorrow!'

Lucy lay back on the grass and stared up at the clouds. It was really weird, but for a moment, the white fluff kind of looked like an aeroplane, with white lofty wings jutting out into the blue sky.

Lucy sighed. She was really looking forward to the performance – the Angels had the best dance routine in the world.

But when tomorrow came, and the Angels performed in front of the entire school, it also meant something else. Something that would happen right after the show.

There would be a real aeroplane taking her big sister away.

CHAPTER

Seven

'Should I check what you've packed?'

Lucy could hear her mum and Frankie talking as she dumped her bag in the hallway. She tiptoed towards the kitchen and peeked through the door.

Her mum and Frankie were sitting next to each other on the stools in the kitchen.

'Mum, you've checked my luggage about a thousand times,' Frankie said.

'Hmmm,' her mum said nervously. 'As long as you haven't forgotten anything major, you'll be fine.'

Lucy could tell by her mum's voice that she was reassuring herself as much as Frankie. 'But we'll miss you, Frankie,' her mum said softly.

Frankie wiggled her nose. It was something she always did when she was nervous. It had started when she and Lucy used to watch *Bewitched* together. Lucy tried to do it too, but she had to use her fingers to wiggle her nose.

Lucy sighed. It was hard to imagine that she wouldn't be watching any TV with Frankie for a whole year!

'Yeah, well Daniel will miss me,' Frankie said softly. Lucy rolled her eyes. Daniel was Frankie's icky boyfriend.

'And you and dad will miss me. And maybe the cat will ...' Frankie continued in a quiet voice.

'Aren't you forgetting someone?' her

mum asked. 'Someone a bit smaller than you?' she prompted.

'Someone-who-is-a-bit-smaller-than-me kicked me out of the playroom yesterday,' Frankie replied. 'I wanted to spend some time with her before I left, but the small one obviously wanted to be alone with her friends . . .'

Lucy froze. Did Frankie really think that she wouldn't miss her? She'd been so stupid! She didn't even realise that Frankie had been hanging around with the Angels so she could spend more time with *her*.

Lucy closed her eyes, and thought hard. She had to be brave. She had to march into the kitchen right now and talk to Frankie. She might even be able to say sorry, although that was a pretty hard thing to say. At least she would be able to explain that she *was* going to miss her.

Lucy took a deep breath. She stepped into the kitchen. But the loud honk of a horn sounded right at that moment. Lucy sighed – icky Daniel had come to pick up Frankie.

'Don't be late, sweetie,' Lucy's mum called after Frankie. 'We have a big day tomorrow.'

'OK, mum,' Frankie responded. As Frankie pushed past Lucy in the corridor, she gave her a little wink. 'Nice spying, small one,' she whispered.

As Lucy watched her sister go, she had a horrible feeling that Frankie *would* be late home, and Lucy would probably be fast asleep by then. That would mean that icky Daniel would be the only person who spoke to Frankie for the rest of the night.

Suddenly, Lucy shuddered. Icky Daniel was probably going to the airport with them tomorrow, too. They were leaving straight after the performance tomorrow.

So Lucy wouldn't get a single chance to be alone with Frankie. She would not get a single chance to tell her sister how she *really* felt.

CHAPTER Eight

It had been a crazy morning. Lucy's mum had forgotten to put peanut butter on her toast. Her dad kept moving Frankie's bags, eventually stacking them all in a pile near the kitchen door, where Lucy kept on tripping over them.

Frankie was still in bed, which wasn't unusual. Lucy had tried to wait up for her last night, but Frankie was just too late.

Lucy pulled on her pink shoes, and checked herself in the mirror on top of her dressing table. As she opened the top drawer to get out her necklace, she spotted her diary. She picked it up and popped it in her school bag. It would be good to write in it straight after the performance. Lucy found it was always good to write things down while they were still fresh in her mind.

Lucy took one last glance in the mirror. Then she picked up her bag, and headed towards the front door.

'Good luck, honey,' her mum called.

Lucy checked the time. If she didn't hurry, she was going to be late. The performances were going to be held first thing in the morning in the multi-purpose room. Lucy shivered. The entire school was going to be there. The entire school was going to be watching the Angels do their thing!

'Break a leg, Lou,' her dad yelled.

'Thanks ... I think, ' she called as she ran past him and out of the house.

The moment she walked through the school gates, Lucy was swamped by the other Angels. It was funny to see all the kids in her grade out of uniform and in their costumes.

The Devils looked really funny in their huge baggy jeans and giant T-shirts. Fake

There are some cool costumes

gold chains clinked around Luke's neck as he approached the Angels.

'Yo,' he said, making a cutting motion with his hand. '*You Angels think you're the best ever born, but you ain't got nothing on the Devils' horns!*'

The Angels looked at each other,

giggling. Then, Bonnie walked up to Luke, her arms crossed in front of her and her chest puffed out.

'*You Devils have got the whole thing wrong, just wait till you hear the Angels' song,*' she rapped.

Lucy cracked up with the other Angels, and Luke swaggered back to the rest of his team.

Soon, the Devils' chant was ringing out for the gazillionth time.

'We're the Devils, just beware!
We will beat you anywhere!
On the ground or in the air,
Devils! Devils! Yeah, yeah, yeah!'

On the last *yeah*, Luke jumped high in the air. He looked back at the Angels, his eyes crossed and his tongue poked out.

'Devils! Devils! Gross, gross, gross!' Bonnie yelled out, mimicking the tune perfectly. Then, she pulled a face that was even funnier than Luke's. She rolled her eyes right back in her head so you could only see the whites of her eyes.

Lucy started cracking up again. But suddenly she realised something shocking. Her face fell and she could feel her heart bumping hard against her rib cage.

The CD! She had forgotten the CD!

Lucy froze, and went very pale.

'What's wrong?' Lola asked.

Lucy just shook her head. How could she have been so dumb? After all the work they'd done? She felt as though she was a rag doll, and someone had taken all the stuffing out of her.

'What is it, Lou?' Bonnie said urgently.

'The CD,' Lucy squeaked. 'It's in the pocket of my school skirt. *At home!*'

Lucy's eyes were wide as she stared at the others. She imagined them being furious with her. When Chloe opened her mouth to speak, Lucy expected her to be really annoyed.

'It's OK, Luce,' Chloe said. 'Everyone makes mistakes.'

Lucy took a deep breath. 'I'm so sorry,' she said shakily.

Chloe tilted her head to the side. 'You can apologise later,' she said with a smile. 'Right now, we'd better hurry. We'll call your parents and ask them to bring the CD to school, all right?'

Lucy was in a trance as she walked with the other Angels to the school office.

Everything was going wrong and it was all her fault. But she just hoped, desperately, that her mum or dad would answer the phone, and bring the CD in before the Angels had to go on stage. But it was probably hopeless. They were probably already on their way to the performance.

Lucy watched in a daze as Chloe got permission to use the phone. She shook her head. She had to snap out of it! Right now! She had to fix her mistake, somehow.

Lucy took a deep breath and punched in her dad's mobile number. After a pause, it started ringing. Lucy's stomach churned.

Chloe nudged her. 'Is he answering?' she asked worriedly.

Lucy shook her head. 'It's ringing out.'

'Try your mum's phone,' Chloe urged.

But Lucy's mum didn't answer her phone either.

'There's only one number left to try,' Lucy whispered, feeling sick.

Lucy's hand shook as she picked up the phone and dialled her home number.

CHAPTER Nine

'Sorry we're not here to take your call right now, but please leave a message after the beep.'

Lucy groaned. The answering machine! This was a disaster.

She waited as the machine beeped about twenty times. They would all be messages from Frankie's friends, saying goodbye.

Finally, it was Lucy's turn.

'Mum, dad ... Frankie?' she began. 'It's Lucy. If you're there ... if you're there, can one of you *please* get the CD out of the pocket of my school skirt? I think it's on the floor in my bedroom. It's really important. Can *someone* run it down to the school, really, really quickly? *Please*. It's —'

Lucy sighed as the answering machine cut her off.

'OK girls, back to the multi-purpose room right now,' Mrs Clarke said, popping her head into the office. 'The Devils are already on stage. Go!'

Lucy's heart was really heavy as she walked with the Angels over to the multi-purpose room. She could hear peals of laughter as they walked inside.

The younger kids were all at the very front, looking up at the stage. They were giggling madly at something the Devils had just done.

Lucy picked her way over to a spot on the floor, hurrying so she wouldn't block the view of the kids behind her for too long. Then she looked up at the stage.

Joey spoke into the microphone. He looked really different in his rap clothes. His jeans were so big that Lucy wondered whether they were about to fall down.

'Ms Diamond, she loves to give out stickers,
But I got so many,
I have to put them on my knickers!'

The audience cracked up as Joey turned around. His underpants were showing above his jeans, and they were entirely covered with stickers!

Lucy was too nervous to laugh along. But she watched as Luke grabbed the microphone from Joey.

'*Mr Paul, he rocks, he ain't no bore,*
But we think his tracksuits are against the law!
Colour co-ordinated right up to his cap,
And now we're finished with our Teacher Rap!'

Applause exploded around the hall. Lucy stared at the huge cardboard clap-o-meter on the side of the stage. Mr Paul was twisting a handle on the back of it and swinging a giant red needle between the numbers, from one to five. The needle wobbled and inched its way towards the four. It hovered and then moved past the four as the clapping and cheering grew even louder.

But suddenly, the sound of laughter drowned out the claps and cheers – Mr Paul had broken the clap-o-meter! The needle had snapped and fallen to the floor, leaving a sheepish Mr Paul holding just the handle!

'Well, I guess we have to say that the Devils' Teacher Rap was pretty popular,' Mr Paul laughed. 'Though I can't think why!'

The crowd roared again as the Devils all bowed behind Mr Paul.

Lucy squinted in the darkness at a clock on the wall. It was no good. The Angels were supposed to go on next. They would just have to do the dance without the music.

Suddenly, Lucy felt a tap on her shoulder. When she looked around, she saw a dark figure reaching out to her. She could just make out a familiar pyjama sleeve, and then even more familiar purple fingernails, holding out ... her CD!

'Frankie!' she yelled.

CHAPTER Ten

'I can't believe that in one minute we're going to be dancing in front of the whole school,' Sophie said nervously, as the Angels gathered at the side of the stage.

'You'll be fine, Soph,' Lucy said. 'We'll all be fine. But there's just one more thing,' Lucy added, handing out some little metal charms. 'Frankie got us all a star for our bracelets.'

Lola giggled as she took hers. 'Because we're stars!' she said.

Sophie helped Lucy with her charm. 'Maybe we should do the hair thing that Frankie showed us after all?' she said quietly to Lucy.

'Great idea!' Lucy grinned. The other Angels nodded happily.

Suddenly, the music rang out across the hall, and the girls leaped onto the stage.

Lucy looked down into the crowd. Frankie was sitting right in the middle of the front row, with all the little kids! Lucy smiled at her and gave her a quick wave. Frankie's eyes shone with pride.

And then the Angels danced.

Lucy felt the music pump through her veins as she moved. She saw the other Angels twist and turn and throw their hair back dramatically. Everyone was moving perfectly as one. She saw kids in the audience leaning forward for a better view of the stage.

Then, she stopped thinking of anything

other than the dance and the music. And she had the best fun she'd had in her entire life. Ever!

As the music faded, the hall was completely silent for a second. The Angels stayed on stage. Lucy felt as though they'd all been frozen into icicles. No-one moved.

Then the clapping began. It started softly, as though people were still too surprised by the dance to clap. But then, it grew louder and louder. Soon, kids were thumping their feet on the floor as well as clapping!

The Angels looked at each other, grinning madly. Then they turned to the audience and waved goodbye.

Lucy grinned. If the clap-o-meter hadn't broken, the Angels would definitely have seen the needle go even higher than it had after the Devils' performance! But Lucy didn't need a clap-o-meter to know that the Angels had done something really special.

As they walked off stage, Lucy took another look in the front row. Frankie's spot was empty. Lucy's heart lurched in her chest. She was going to have to get used to Frankie not being there – not being anywhere nearby – and for a whole year! Lucy swallowed and took a deep breath. She reminded herself that Frankie probably had hundreds of things to do before they left for the airport that afternoon. Like change out of her pyjamas, for instance!

'Hey, we'd better go back to our seats,' Chloe said, beaming at Lucy. 'The Super Stars are on in five minutes.'

'I'll be there in a sec,' Lucy replied, grabbing her bag, and feeling around for her diary. Even if Lucy didn't get a chance to talk to Frankie before she left, she *was* going to the airport to see her off. And she *was* going to make sure Frankie knew how she felt.

There was going to be a surprise tucked into her hand luggage.

Lucy smiled at Chloe as she took her pen and diary out of her bag.

'You go, Chloe. I'll be there in a sec. There's something I have to do first.'

Dear Frankie,

This is a special note for a very special big sister. I hope you've found it in your handbag while you're on the plane because I want you to know exactly how I feel before you get to Spain.

I'm going to miss you like crazy! I'm missing you already, and you haven't even gone yet! It's going to be so weird without you in the house. You're the best big sister in the universe. Promise me you'll email me, OK?

And one other thing — thanks for helping the Angels. I hope you noticed that we did the hair thing, just like you showed us! I think we totally rocked the performance thanks to you!

I promise that I will call you as soon as possible.

Love always,

The small one x x

P.S. GO ANGELS!!!

The End

COMING UP...

GO GIRL! Angels

It has been full-on working together on the Team Terrific challenges. The Angels have managed to become more than a team – they're like besties! But what happens when it's all over?

ANGELS FOREVER